# 5-Minute Classic Tales

sequoia
children's publishing

# Huckleberry Finn

*Original Story by Mark Twain   Adapted by Virginia Biles   Illustrated by Linda Dockey Graves*

I am Huck Finn. You know about me if you have read *The Adventures of Tom Sawyer* by Mr. Mark Twain. In that book, Tom and I found a lot of money. Judge Thatcher put the money in the bank to keep it safe for us. Since everyone thought my Pap was dead, the Widow Douglas took me to raise. She was good to me, but she made me wear proper clothes and sleep in a bed.

Pap heard about the money and came back to town to get it, but Judge Thatcher would not let him have it. Pap took me across the river to a cabin. When he left, he locked me in. I got out and decided to run away. I killed a wild pig with an ax and spread the blood all over the cabin. I pulled some of my hair out and stuck it on the ax blade. Then I dumped the dead pig in the river. I found an old rowboat and rowed to Jackson's Island.

On the island, I stumbled on someone by a campfire. It was Jim, Miss Watson's slave. "What are you doing here, Jim?" I asked.

"Promise you won't tell, Huck," Jim said. "I've run away. Miss Watson is going to sell me to a slave dealer. He's going to take me to a plantation down South. I don't want to leave my family!"

I knew it was wrong to help a runaway slave, but I could not tell on Jim without people knowing I was not dead.

"I won't tell, Jim," I said.

While we were on the island, the Mississippi River flooded, and we saw a house floating in it. We went out to it, climbed in through a window, and found all kinds of useful things inside. Another day, we found a raft floating down the river. We pulled it to shore and hid it in the bushes.

Another day, I wanted to know who they thought had killed me. So no one would recognize me, I put on a dress and a bonnet we found in the floating house. I rowed across the river and knocked on the door of a cabin. A woman answered and invited me in. "What's your name?" she asked me.

"Mary Williams," I said.

She looked at me funny. Then she talked about Huck Finn getting killed.

"We think that slave Jim killed him and is hiding on Jackson's Island," she said. "My husband went to find some men to go over there with him. What did you say your name was?"

"Sarah Williams," I said.

"I thought you said it was Mary Williams," she said.

Just then, a rat ran across the floor. The woman tossed me a lump of coal, and I caught it in one hand. She told me to hit the rat. I threw the coal so hard the rat was dead in a second.

"You throw just like a boy," she said. "Tell me who you really are."

I got out of there as fast as I could and rowed back to Jim. We had to get off the island before the men came looking for us. "Jim," I called. "They're after us!"

We piled our things on the raft and shoved off down the Mississippi. We planned to take Jim to the Ohio River. He could go up the Ohio River to free country. To hide from slave hunters, we tied the raft to a tree and hid it with tree branches during the day. Then we fished and slept until it grew dark. At night, we tied a lantern to a pole in the middle of the raft and rode along and talked or just looked up at the stars. Sometimes I slept, and Jim took my turn watching for boats.

It was wonderful living on the raft, but my conscience was really bothering me. I was helping a slave escape. I knew I had to slip ashore and tell on Jim.

"I'm going ashore for news," I said one night and started off in the rowboat.

"There you go, Huck!" Jim called out to me. "You're the only friend Jim has!"

Another rowboat pulled up beside me. Two men were in it. "We're looking for a runaway slave," one man said. "Who's on your raft? Black or white?"

"It's my Pap," I lied. "He's really sick. I think it's smallpox. Come help me."

They backed their boat away from mine. They put some coins on a piece of wood and shoved it toward me. "You go on down the river, boy," one man said.

I went back to Jim. I could not turn him in.

We had lots of adventures floating down the Mississippi. Then we missed the Ohio River and went deeper into slave territory. Jim was in danger all the time.

One day we picked up two raggedy-looking men who called themselves the King and the Duke. They were not really royalty, but we treated them like they were. That made them happy, and it did not hurt us any. They had a scheme to make money by putting on a play. They did *Romeo and Juliet*. The Duke was Juliet, and he looked silly pretending to be a girl because he had long white whiskers. The play was so terrible, the audiences threw rotten tomatoes at them.

Later, they learned that a man named Peter Wilks had died. They pretended to be Peter's relatives. The King pretended to be a preacher from England, and the Duke pretended to be his deaf brother. They made me be their servant, but my English accent was terrible.

Peter Wilks had left most of his money to his two nieces, but the King and the Duke took it. Before they could leave, I stole the money back and hid it in Peter's coffin. I really liked Miss Mary Jane, the older girl. I did not want to see those old frauds cheat the girls. After the body was buried, I told Miss Mary Jane where the money was hidden. The King and the Duke did not know what I had done.

Another day, we stopped at a little river town. I went into a printer's shop and had a poster made offering a reward for the return of a slave named Jim. If we were stopped, I could say I had captured Jim and was returning him to his owner. I thought that was a good plan. It turned out to be not so good.

A few days later, I went into another little town to get supplies, and when I got back to the raft, Jim was gone. The King and the Duke had turned him in for the "reward." Some farmers had agreed to pay them half of the "reward" money. All the farmers had to do, they thought, was turn Jim in to his owner. They would wait until the owner came and paid them the full reward.

They had taken Jim to the Phelps farm. I did not know what to do. No owner was coming for Jim, and there was no reward money. I decided I would write a letter to Miss Watson back in Petersburg and tell her where Jim was. Jim would still be a slave, but he would be back with people he knew instead of on the Phelps farm. I knew Miss Watson would be angry with Jim for running away and people would know that Huck Finn was not dead, but I had to write the letter.

Then I remembered all the good times Jim and I had coming down the river. I remembered how Jim stood my watch for me. I remembered how Jim considered me his friend. I knew if I did not turn Jim in, I was going to the bad place when I died. I did not want that, but Jim was more like my father than Pap ever was.

"I'll go to the bad place," I said, and I tore up the letter.

The next morning, I started out for the Phelps farm. When I got close, five dogs started barking at me. Then the door opened, and an old man and woman ran out and started hugging and kissing me.

"Tom Sawyer," the old woman said, "we thought you'd never get here! Why are you so late? How's my sister?"

After a minute, I figured out she thought I was my friend Tom Sawyer from Petersburg. Tom lived with his Aunt Polly, but this was his other aunt and uncle. I just let them think I was Tom. Then I remembered Tom would be coming! I had to stop him.

"I'm going to get my bag," I said and hurried up the road.

When Tom saw me, he thought I was a ghost!

"I'm not a ghost, Tom. I'm really Huck, and I really need your help," I said.

I told him about Jim being held at the Phelps place and how I was going to free him and go on down the river.

"I'll help!" Tom said. "I'll pretend to be my brother. We'll tell Aunt Sally and Uncle Silas my visit is a surprise."

That night, we climbed out of the bedroom window and looked around until we found Jim. He was locked up in an old shed, and he was really glad to see us.

"Let's steal the key from Uncle Silas," I said.

"That doesn't have style," Tom said. "It has to be like in the storybooks."

Tom liked to read about kings and dukes. I had had enough of royalty, but Tom had his way. That night, we climbed out the window and ran for the shed. We dug a tunnel under the shed, large enough for Jim to crawl through.

"Crawl out, Jim," I called.

Just as Jim's head and shoulders came out of the hole, we saw a lantern light on the porch of the house.

"Who's there?" called Uncle Silas. "Stop or I'll shoot."

Jim pulled himself out of the hole, and the three of us ran for the fence. I heard a *crack*. Tom was hit, but he was happy because he had a bullet in his leg! Tom wanted Jim to run for the river, but Jim would not go.

"You wouldn't leave me, and I'm not going to leave you," Jim said. "Huck, you go for the doctor. I'll stay here with Tom."

I went to town and found a doctor and took him to Tom. Tom was really sick with a fever, but the doctor saved him. The next morning, the doctor and Jim carried Tom back to the Phelps farm. Aunt Sally was really happy to see Tom alive. She put him to bed, and I sat by him.

"Did Jim get away?" Tom asked when he finally woke up.

"No," I said. "He helped save your life. He's locked up in the shed again."

Before I could tell him any more, the bedroom door opened. There was Tom's Aunt Sally with Aunt Polly from Petersburg! I dove under the bed.

"Come out from there, Huck Finn!" Aunt Polly said.

"That's not Huck Finn. That's Tom," Aunt Sally said, pointing at me.

"That's Huck Finn," Aunt Polly said. "That rascal in bed is Tom."

I was caught! Jim was caught, too. Aunt Sally told Aunt Polly that the men were coming to hang Jim. He was a runaway slave who had tried to escape.

"Jim's free," Tom said. "Miss Watson freed him in her will when she died."

"Miss Watson died?" I asked.

"While you were pretending to be dead, Miss Watson died," Aunt Polly said.

Jim was free! He went back to Petersburg to be near his family. Tom went back to Petersburg with Aunt Polly, wearing the bullet from his leg on a watch chain. Aunt Sally wanted to adopt me, but I was not ready to wear proper clothes and sleep in a bed. I had more adventures ahead of me.

# Call of the Wild

*Original Story by Jack London    Adapted by Elizabeth Olson    Illustrated by Jane Maday*

Buck lives in the sunny Southland at Judge Miller's place. From a shady spot near the driveway, Buck can watch over the judge's property. He can see the wide lawn and the clear pool. Far in the distance, he can see the outlines of the orchards and woods.

Buck has a good life. He spends his days enjoying the Southland's fine weather. He rolls in the grass. He jumps into the refreshing pool. He runs from the tip of the driveway to the far reaches of the woods. Without stopping to rest, he doubles back and returns to the house. His strong legs never tire. In the evenings, when the air is cooler, Buck lies at the judge's feet near the fire in the house.

Many people live on Judge Miller's place. A dozen gardeners tend the lawns and the trees. Another dozen house maids clean and cook in the house.

Many animals live on Judge Miller's place, too. Behind the stable, a pack of fox terriers lives in a kennel. They help Judge Miller hunt in the fall. A few small dogs live in the house. Buck thinks they are strange. The small dogs never even stick their noses outside to sniff the fresh air.

Buck is neither kennel dog nor house dog. He goes where he pleases and does what he likes. His manner shows he is his own master.

One day, from his spot near the driveway, Buck sees one of the gardeners.

"Hello, Buck," says the gardener.

Buck stands and wags his tail. The man reaches down to pat Buck's head. As he does so, he slips a rope around Buck's neck. Buck feels it tighten. He gasps.

"I'm going to sell you," says the gardener. "Judge Miller is away until next week. He won't know you're missing until he returns."

The gardener pulls on the rope. Unable to resist, Buck follows. The gardener leads Buck down through the orchard and into the woods. They stop at the railroad station at the wood's edge. Buck recognizes it as the place where workers load the judge's apples onto trains. Buck looks around for fruit. There is none. Instead, he sees a stranger with a large cage.

"He is a strong dog," says the stranger. "He'll do well in the Northland."

"His name is Buck," says the gardener. "Take good care of him."

The gardener gives the rope to the stranger. Buck growls. The stranger gives some money to the gardener.

"Don't worry, Buck," says the stranger. "Just step into this cage."

The stranger tugs on the rope. Buck tries to resist, but the stranger pulls harder on the rope. Buck steps into the cage. The stranger quickly removes the rope from Buck's neck, closes the cage door, and locks it.

"You're going on a long journey," says the stranger as he shuts the door.

Alone and in the dark, Buck feels the train move forward.

The train speeds along. Buck does not recognize his surroundings.

"This isn't the Southland," thinks Buck. "The sun is less bright, and it's colder."

"Poor Buck," says the conductor. "You're shivering. I'll put some hay in your crate, but you'll have to get used to the cold. You're going to the Northland."

Buck welcomes the hay. He crawls into it to keep warm.

One day, the train chugs to a stop. The conductor opens Buck's cage. Buck hears and sees the dogs. Hundreds of them are in an open field. They are all shapes and colors. They seem to be everywhere, jumping, running, playing, eating, or sleeping.

Buck jumps from the train car. His feet sink into something white and cold on the ground. He springs backward with surprise. He sniffs at it.

"This must be your first snow," says the conductor.

When night falls, Buck feels the air turn bitter cold. He looks for the conductor and his cage with the warm hay, but the train is gone. Buck shivers in the snow.

"You must be new here," says a friendly voice.

Buck looks up and sees a big yellow dog.

"My name is Dave," says the yellow dog. "Just dig a hole in the snow and climb inside. You'll be warm all night."

"My name is Buck," he says. "Thanks very much for the help."

The next morning, Buck wakes in darkness. He does not know where he is. He bolts upward from his snowy bed, and sunshine hits his face.

"There you are, Buck," says a man wearing a hat with a tassel. "You belong to me now. You will help me deliver the mail to the country's interior. Have some breakfast before we hit the trail."

The man holds a piece of meat toward Buck. Buck likes the man's kind face and gentle manner. He eagerly takes the food.

After breakfast, the man in the tasseled hat leads Buck to a sled. He fastens an arrangement of straps and buckles to him. Buck feels like the horses at Judge Miller's place. The man fastens some dogs in front of Buck and one behind him. Buck does not know what to do. He feels the pull of the strap and becomes afraid.

"Don't worry, Buck," says the dog behind him, "I'll tell you what to do."

Buck turns and sees Dave, the big yellow dog.

Suddenly, the man yells, "Mush!"

All of the dogs strain, and the sled moves forward. The experience is new and strange. Buck is embarrassed about having to do the work of a horse, but he pulls the sled with all his might. A quick learner, Buck soon pulls the sled as well as the other dogs.

For many weeks, the sled team travels across the Northland. On the sled are two heavy mailbags. The man with the tasseled hat and his dogs work hard.

Buck learns how to live in the Northland. Dave shows Buck how to bite the ice out with his teeth when it collects between his toes. He shows Buck how to break the ice on the top of the water dish by striking it with a paw.

Over time, Buck's senses grow sharper. He learns to smell the wind in order to choose the best spot for his bed. He becomes so good at predicting the direction of the wind that he always chooses a spot that remains free of the wind all night.

Buck does have one problem. His feet are not as hard as those of the other dogs. He limps in agony from the long days on the trail. One night, he cannot even rise to receive his ration of meat.

The man sets the meat near Buck's hungry mouth. While Buck eats, the man massages Buck's sore paws.

The next day, the man puts four tiny shoes on Buck's feet. Buck runs with the shoes, and his feet no longer hurt. After a while the shoes fall off, but by then Buck no longer needs them. His feet are tough enough for the trail.

Buck likes pulling the sled with the other dogs. He takes pride in the hard work. At the end of the day, he feels good even though he is very tired.

The man with the tasseled hat drives the sled across plains and riverbeds. The dogs run in deep snow and on slick ice. Sometimes the ice cracks beneath their feet, and the man drives them forward as fast as possible. He does not allow them to stop because the weight of the sled would pull them through the ice.

One day along the Thirty Mile River, the team crosses a patch of very thin ice. The lead dog, Spitz, breaks through it. He plunges into the water. The harness quickly pulls the next three dogs into the hole after him.

Buck and Dave strain with all their might. Their paws slip and fly, but they move back slowly. The man pulls the dogs from the water. They are coated with ice.

"We must build a fire," says the man. "Buck and Dave, find wood!"

Buck and Dave dig into the snow. Soon they each have large sticks in their mouths. The man uses the wood to build a fire. The cold, wet dogs run around the hot flames in circles. The ice melts from their bodies. Soon they are dry and warm.

The dogs are grateful for Buck and Dave's help. The man is grateful, too.

Buck likes the other dogs, especially Dave. Almost all of them like him, too. Buck's strength, speed, and survival skills make him a valuable member of the sled team. His manner, well known at Judge Miller's place, makes him stand out. Spitz, the lead dog, is threatened by Buck.

One night while Buck is eating his ration of meat, he looks up at the beautiful moon. When he looks down again, his meat is gone. Spitz is greedily eating it.

"That wasn't a good idea," says Buck. "Next time you won't be so lucky."

"You're no match for me," says Spitz. "I'm the lead dog. I do what I want."

A few nights later, Buck leaves his cozy sleeping spot for a drink of water. When he returns to his bed, he discovers Spitz in it.

"I warned you," says Buck.

"I can do what I want," says Spitz. "I'm the strongest dog on the team."

"Not anymore," says Buck.

In a flash, the two dogs pounce on one another. In a matter of seconds, Spitz proves to be no match for Buck's strength and speed. With a bruised body and hurt dignity, Spitz slinks away. Buck is now the lead dog.

Buck leads the team across the Northland. His instincts become sharp. If he catches the scent of a bear on the wind, he knows to direct the sled away from it. If the team loses control of the sled going downhill, Buck knows to run toward an incline. The man trusts Buck's instincts and follows him.

As in his earlier life, Buck again carries himself as if he is his own master. He goes where he pleases and does what he pleases. But unlike before, Buck now prefers to be with the man and to work for him. He helps the man deliver the mail to the interior of the country in record time. After only a few days of rest, the team begins the return trip. All the dogs are eager to hit the trail.

Buck remembers the judge and his former home. He recalls the days spent at the end of the driveway. He remembers rolling in the grass and diving into the pool. He thinks of the fox terriers and the house dogs. He misses the Southland sometimes, but he loves the Northland.

One night, Buck joins the other dogs in the darkness beyond the man's fire. Together the dogs howl at the moon. They call out to the spirits of their ancestors who pulled the sleds of long ago. Buck even thinks he can see his ancestors' paw prints. He imagines that he is following an ancient path.

Buck knows that his new life is the right life for him. With joy, he lifts his head to the full moon and howls.

# King Arthur

*Original Story by Sir Thomas Malory    Adapted by Jamie Elder    Illustrated by Edward V. Kadunc*

Uther Pendragon was king and overlord of the entire realm of Britain. He was very powerful, but he often listened to his friend and advisor, Merlin the Wise. Merlin was a good advisor who also knew great magic and could foretell the future.

One day, a son was born to Uther Pendragon. On that same day, Merlin foresaw the king's death in a vision.

"I am not afraid to die," said Uther Pendragon after learning of Merlin's vision, "but my son is not safe."

To keep the baby safe, Merlin took him away to be raised in secret. Soon after, Uther Pendragon died in battle.

Britain became a place of chaos after the death of Uther Pendragon because it was believed he had no heir. The lords of the land fought among themselves. Each believed he could claim the throne for himself if there was no heir. The chaos lasted for eighteen years.

When the lords finally asked for his help, Merlin knew what to do. He announced a contest to bring the lords and their sons to one place. The winner of the contest would be the true king of the entire realm of Britain. Merlin just hoped that eighteen years was long enough for Uther Pendragon's son to have grown into a man.

All the lords and their sons stopped fighting among themselves when they heard about the contest. Each wanted to prove himself to be the true king of Britain, so they all went to the place appointed by Merlin.

The place was a clearing with room for many men. In the center of the clearing, Merlin caused a great stone to appear. Upon the stone, he caused a mighty anvil to appear. And in that anvil, he caused a sword to be struck deep into the center.

That sword was a very special sword. It was like lightning with a hilt of gold and a cross set with blue stones. It was the sword of Uther Pendragon, and the man who could pull it free would prove himself to be the king's son and heir.

Men came from all parts of Britain, but no one knew what to expect. Merlin would not announce the object of the contest until every man had arrived. To keep them from becoming too curious, he called for a tournament-at-arms.

Sir Ector arrived just as the tournament was announced. Sir Ector was a great lord, and with him were his two sons. His elder son was Sir Kay, and his younger son was Arthur.

Sir Kay was dark and handsome and very brave. He was a knight of great valor.

Arthur was fair and bright and served as esquire-at-arms to Sir Kay. He brought great honor to his brother.

Sir Kay asked his father's permission to join the tournament, and Sir Ector gave it. Sir Kay went, and Arthur led him to the battlefield with spear and pennant.

When both sides of the battlefield were ready to charge upon one another, Arthur kept track of Sir Kay. As one side met the other, Arthur did not lose sight of Sir Kay. When the assault was over, Arthur ran to Sir Kay to attend to him.

Sir Kay was pleased with his abilities on the battlefield. He had fought well and had overcome many of his foes. He was still upon his own horse without a scratch. Yet in a violent charge, his sword had broken in two.

"I shall find another sword for your use," said Arthur to his brother.

Arthur ran to find his father's sword, but his father was nowhere to be found. Arthur debated, but he knew he could not take his father's sword without permission. He would have to find another sword.

Arthur ran quickly, and soon he came to a wide clearing. In the center of the clearing he saw an unclaimed sword in a mighty anvil upon a great stone.

Arthur did not think twice about how such a thing could be. He could only see the beauty of the sword that was there. It was like lightning with a hilt of gold and a cross set with blue stones. It felt right to him that he should take it.

Arthur held the sword aloft and ran back to the battlefield. He presented it to his brother, and Sir Kay was pleased.

Sir Kay went into the second assault and did as well as he had done in the first. When the tournament battle was over, he rode toward his father and brother. With them was Merlin, and all three of them looked happy.

"You have done honor to your family," said Sir Ector to Sir Kay.

"Yes," said Merlin. "And you have the honor of a great sword."

Sir Kay looked at the precious sword and feared Arthur had stolen it without meaning to. Sir Kay wanted to protect his brother from any undue punishment.

"I was in need of one after the first assault," said Sir Kay. "I did not mean to have it taken from its rightful owner."

"Do you know, then, to whom it rightfully belongs?" asked Merlin.

"I do not," said Sir Kay, "but it can be returned."

"You cannot return it," said Merlin.

"Sir Kay did not take the sword," said Arthur. "I took it. I did not believe it belonged to anyone, and my brother was in need of it. I will take my punishment as it is due. I would not want to bring dishonor upon my family."

Merlin took the sword, wrapped it in a fold of his bright tunic, and went toward his tent. Sir Ector steered Arthur away from the crowd. Sir Kay followed behind. Inside Merlin's tent, they were quiet for a long time.

"I should be punished," said Arthur. "I did not think before I took the sword. It felt right to do so, and I cannot explain that."

"I would like to explain it to you," said Merlin.

Merlin took the sword from his tunic and held it out to Arthur. Arthur looked at the sword for a long time.

"It is with this sword that you shall bring honor to your family name. It belongs to you. The anvil and the stone were the contest meant to prove your ownership."

"That is the contest, then," said Sir Ector. "I am glad it has happened this way. I am glad to be here as Arthur is told. Arthur is my son, but I am no longer his father."

"My brother," protested Sir Kay, "shall not be disowned over a misunderstanding!"

"It is you who misunderstands," said Sir Ector. "Please listen as Merlin explains it. It is a very simple matter, but I have been quiet on the subject too long to do it justice now."

"You understand this sword," Merlin said to Arthur.

"It seems familiar, although I have never seen it," said Arthur.

"Then it is as it should be," said Merlin. "This sword belonged to your father."

Arthur looked at Sir Ector, but Sir Ector shook his head.

"Sir Ector has been like a father to you, but he is not your father," said Merlin.

"Sir Ector shall always be my father," Arthur said, "but I understand what you mean. If you say I am the son of another, I believe you. Who, then, is my father?"

"Your father was Uther Pendragon," Merlin said. "On the day of your birth, I foresaw he would not live long. He knew men would fight to control Britain, and he feared for your safety. I took you away for your safety."

"You took me to Sir Ector," said Arthur.

"I had one son," said Sir Ector. "Then I had two. It was my honor to raise you and to watch you grow beside your brother."

"When you were safely away, men did indeed fight to control the realm of Britain," said Merlin. "It has been a long time of chaos. I hoped it would only last long enough for you to become a man. So it did, and so you have."

Arthur felt Sir Kay trembling at his side. Sir Kay would not look at him, so Arthur put his hand on his brother's shoulder.

"Now the lords have asked for my help," continued Merlin. "I planned for this contest long ago."

"Why have a contest?" asked Arthur.

"It will not be obvious to all men that you are the rightful heir to the throne of Britain," said Merlin. "It must be proven twice. I set the sword in the anvil upon the stone, and only the true heir can claim it. Each man will realize he is not the king if he cannot take the sword. In turn, he will realize you are the true king when you take it so easily."

"So tomorrow, it shall be proven that I am the king," said Arthur.

"That was proven today," said Merlin. "It was proven to you. Tomorrow it shall be proven to all the lords and their sons."

Sir Kay made a noise beside Arthur.

"We will always be brothers," Arthur said to comfort him.

Sir Kay looked upon the man he knew as his brother but who was now a king. He tried to speak, but he could not. In frustration, he fled from the tent.

Sir Kay was nowhere to be found that night or the next morning when it was time to go to the contest. Arthur and Sir Ector went to the gathering place without him. When Merlin saw them arrive, he announced the rules of the contest.

"The man who can pull the sword from this mighty anvil upon this great stone is the true king and overlord of the entire realm of Britain," said Merlin.

In turn, each of the lords and all their sons tried to pull the sword from the anvil. When not one of them could take the sword, an angry noise filled the air.

"No one can take your sword, Merlin!" shouted one of the lords.

"It is not my sword," said Merlin. "It is the sword of Uther Pendragon. Only his rightful heir can claim it!"

Finally, Arthur came forward to the mighty anvil upon the great stone. He gripped the hilt of the sword and easily drew it out. He held the sword high, and the crowd fell silent.

"Is this how you honor your king — with silence?" demanded a voice from the back of the crowd. It was Sir Kay. "You are my king, Arthur Pendragon!" he called out, dropping to one knee.

In suit, every man gathered there dropped to one knee before the king. And from that day forth, all the lords and their sons knew that Arthur was the true king of the entire realm of Britain.

# Treasure Island

*Original Story by Robert Louis Stevenson    Adapted by Graham Wiemer    Illustrated by Victoria and Julius Lisi*

I first set eyes on the ragged old seaman when he came to the Admiral Benbow Inn, dragging a battered sea chest.

"I'm Jim Hawkins," I told him. "My mother and I run this inn."

"You can call me Captain," he said, as I helped him carry his sea chest up to his room. "I'll pay you a silver coin if you keep an eye out for a seaman with one leg. He's a low-down pirate."

Days later, another man came to the inn. I did not alert the captain because the man had both his legs. "I'm looking for Billy Bones," said the burly stranger.

"You've found him, Black Dog!" yelled the captain.

Black Dog and the captain, Billy Bones, went at each other with swords. Black Dog was bested by the captain, and he ran off in defeat.

Later, a blind man came to the inn and gave me a piece of paper. "Take this to Billy Bones," he said.

I gave the paper to the captain.

"This is a warning, Jim," he said. "Black Dog and his men are coming back to take my sea chest. I'm going to hide it here at the inn. Then I'll leave for a while. Black Dog will eventually look for me somewhere else."

The captain went to his room and began to lift up the floorboards. I knew he was hiding the chest under the floor.

"I'm sure there's money in that chest, and Mr. Bones hasn't paid us yet," said my mother. When the captain had gone, we pulled up the floorboards and found the chest. I pried open the lid and found a fortune in silver and gold.

"Take only what he owes us and leave the rest," said my mother.

I grabbed some gold coins, but I could not resist a mysterious paper.

"I'm certain Black Dog and his men are pirates," said my mother. "They'll come for that treasure chest. We must hide!"

We hid in the woods and waited. Then we heard noises coming from the inn.

"They've found the treasure by now!" my mother said. "What else could they be looking for?"

I pulled the paper from my pocket and opened it. Under the light of the moon, I could see it was a treasure map!

"This must be what they're after," I said. "An island is marked on it to show where a treasure is buried."

"You must take that map to Dr. Livesey," said my mother. "He'll know what to do."

Dr. Livesey was our friend, and we trusted him. I walked to his house. I showed him the map and explained what had happened.

"We are the only ones who can find the buried treasure!" Dr. Livesey said excitedly. "If the pirates had another map, they would not need this one. I'll go to the nearest seaport, rent a ship, and hire a crew. You shall be the cabin boy, and we'll sail for this Treasure Island!"

I joined Dr. Livesey at the port of Bristol. He had hired Captain Smollett and a fine ship named the *Hispaniola*. He also hired a one-legged man as the ship's cook. The cook's name was Long John Silver.

Dr. Livesey told me Long John Silver had spent many years at sea. He thought Long John was a fine man, so he hired him. He even hired some of Long John's friends for the crew.

A few days before we sailed, I saw the pirate Black Dog in a tavern. He must have seen me, too, because he left quickly. I asked Long John if he knew Black Dog because it looked to me as if he did. He said he did not, and it made me suspicious.

The crew members who knew Long John seemed to regard him more as a captain than as the cook, which only made me distrust him more. I did not tell Dr. Livesey and Captain Smollett my suspicions because I wanted to be certain.

Only Dr. Livesey, Captain Smollett, and I were supposed to know the purpose of our journey, but several of the crewmen talked openly of the treasure hunt. I suspected Black Dog had told Long John that I had taken the treasure map.

On our first day at sea, I discovered an unusual shipmate. "Pieces of eight! Pieces of eight!" he screeched as I entered the galley.

"Cap'n Flint's his name," Long John said. "He always sails with me."

I later learned why. The parrot served as Long John's lookout.

A few nights later I was having trouble sleeping and decided to go up on deck. I came across a large barrel with a few apples at the bottom. When I heard the click of Long John's wooden leg on the deck, I jumped into the barrel.

The voices of a few other men became clear to me as Long John and his mates drew closer. I hoped they would not see me.

"When do we make our move?" asked one of the men. "I can't take much more of Smollett giving me orders. We should do away with him and his men, now!"

"Arrrr, and what if we can't find the treasure map?" growled Long John. "We'll wait till the treasure is aboard ship before we take care of the captain and his crew."

I no longer had any doubts about Long John Silver. He was a pirate!

I stayed still until I was sure the pirates were gone. Then I got out of the barrel and ran to Dr. Livesey's cabin. He was upset when I told him what I had heard.

"Jim, the first thing we must do is alert the captain," said Dr. Livesey.

We went to Captain Smollett's cabin and told him about Long John's plans.

"We won't be safe if they think we know," said the captain. "Long John brought aboard eighteen men. We can count on only the three of us and four other men."

Luckily, the next few days passed quietly. The pirates never suspected we knew of their scheme. Then, on the sixth day of our voyage, we heard the shout we had been waiting for.

"Land ho!" bellowed the lookout from the crow's nest.

We finally arrived at Treasure Island. The captain let Long John and some of his pirates go ashore in a rowboat. I jumped into it as it pulled away from the ship.

Long John welcomed me aboard, but I could tell he was angry. I told him I was too excited to stay on the ship, but I really wanted to find out more about his plans.

As soon as we landed, I jumped from the rowboat and ran off toward some trees. It would be safer for me to spy on them from a distance.

I saw something moving in the trees, and I froze. It was a man. I feared it was one of the pirates come to harm me.

"What are you doing here?" asked the man.

I could tell by his ragged clothes that he was a seaman who had been on the island a long time. I told him my name and explained how I got there. When I mentioned the name Long John Silver, it upset him.

"Ben Gunn is my name," said the man. "I once served on a ship with Long John Silver, and there is no one who strikes more fear in the hearts of seamen than Long John Silver."

Ben told me he was left on the island three years ago because he knew the ship's captain had buried a fortune on it. The captain figured Ben would not live long enough to tell anyone about it.

Ben also told me about a small boat he had built. Suddenly we heard the pirates approaching, and Ben ran off before I could ask him if he knew where the treasure was buried.

Meanwhile on the *Hispaniola,* as Dr. Livesey told me later, Captain Smollett searched the island through his telescope and discovered a fort. The captain and Dr. Livesey filled a rowboat with food and weapons and headed for the fort with the four loyal crewmen. They figured they would have a better chance against the pirates if they made it to the fort.

Just before the rowboat reached the shore, the pirates still aboard the *Hispaniola* began to fire the ship's cannons at the rowboat.

"Row faster, lads!" yelled the captain. "It's mutiny!"

Soon a cannonball fell near the boat and sank it. No one was hurt, but the men had to wade ashore with the supplies. They knew the sound of the cannons would bring Long John and his pirates to shore, so they had to get to the fort. They made it just in time.

The pirates had managed to smuggle rifles ashore, and shots rang out. But Dr. Livesey knew Long John would have to wait for the pirates who were aboard the *Hispaniola* before he would have the advantage.

I went to the fort to escape the cannon fire. I saw the captain and crew make it inside unharmed. I slipped past the pirates to the southern wall of the fort, and the crewmen recognized me and let me in.

Dr. Livesey was surprised but very glad to see me. I explained everything and told him about Ben Gunn. Just as I finished my story, we heard a voice from outside the fort.

"Smollett!" yelled Long John. "Allow me to approach and speak my piece!"

"I'll listen if you come unarmed and alone," the captain called back.

Long John approached. "You'll be safe if you give up the map," he said.

"If you find that treasure," replied the captain, "no man of mine will be safe."

Long John was mad, but there was nothing he could do by himself without a weapon. He left the fort, limping on his wooden leg.

Gunshots immediately hit the fort. One pirate climbed into a tree and fired a shot that hit the captain. Luckily, the bullet only grazed him. Our return fire chased the pirate down. Long John stopped the attack because he could not take the fort.

Dr. Livesey tended to the captain's wound. Then he took his rifle, climbed the south wall, and ran toward the woods to find Ben Gunn.

When it was dark enough, I found Ben's boat and rowed to the *Hispaniola*. I cut the anchor rope with my knife. The ship would run ashore and give us access to more supplies, so I climbed aboard.

When the ship landed, I went back to the fort. It was dark inside, and I heard a cry as I entered. "Pieces of eight! Pieces of eight!" screeched Long John's parrot. The pirates had taken control of the fort!

"Young Jim!" Long John Silver snarled at me. "The captain handed over the fort and the treasure map, and I let him leave with his men."

The next morning, we set out to find the treasure.

"Shiver me timbers!" bellowed Long John after a few hours. "This is the spot!"

"You've double-crossed us!" one of the pirates said when he saw the hole in the ground. "Smollett took the treasure! You'll divide it with him instead of us!"

Just then, rifle shots whizzed over our heads. The pirates scattered, but Long John remained. Dr. Livesey, Captain Smollett, and Ben Gunn came out of the trees.

Ben explained that he had already found the treasure and hid it in a cave. The captain had given the map to Long John to lure him into a trap, and it worked!

We carried the treasure to the *Hispaniola*. Long John helped, but we watched him. The captain wanted to take him back to England to stand trial for mutiny.

We saw no more of Long John's other pirates. We knew they would rather be stranded on an island than stand trial for mutiny. We left them to fend for themselves and set sail.

At the nearest port, Captain Smollett and Dr. Livesey went ashore to hire a new crew. While they were gone, Long John escaped. We did not go after him because we had the treasure.

When we arrived home, we divided the treasure among us and became very rich men. I was happy to take care of my mother, but the journey to Treasure Island was the best time of my life.

# Pocahontas

*Original Story by Captain John Smith    Adapted by Lisa Harkrader    Illustrated by Karen Pritchett*

Pocahontas!" called my mother. "Stay here by our lodge." When my mother was not looking, I crept away to the edge of the village. I pretended to gather sticks for the fire, but I was really watching the woods.

That morning, a warrior from a neighboring tribe came to talk to my father. Now everyone was talking in low voices. Something was happening, and I did not want to miss it.

Warriors came out of the woods. They were leading a prisoner. It was one of the Englishmen from the strange wooden village by the sea.

The prisoner was odd-looking. A bush of hair sprouted from his face. His skin was pale, but he was not sick. His clothes were made of a strange animal skin, so even-colored that I knew it was not deer skin. He must have been cold because he was not painted with grease to keep warm.

The warriors led him to my father's lodge. My father was the most important man in our tribe. He was chief of the Powhatan, and he ruled many tribes.

I dropped my sticks and followed the warriors.

The Englishman's name was John Smith. Father liked him. He liked the way John Smith looked him in the eye. He liked the way John Smith spoke with a strong voice. He even liked John Smith's strange tools.

John Smith called one of these tools a compass. It was carved from something hard and white, which I thought was bone, but John Smith called it ivory. It was covered with a clear flat stone that John Smith said was glass. Inside, a tiny arrow moved as if by magic. John Smith showed Father how to tell directions with it.

Soon, Father decided it was time for the feast. The women of the tribe brought baskets of fish, corn, pumpkins, melons, and bread. John Smith ate until he could eat no more.

After the feast, the ritual began. Father nodded, and the strongest warriors grabbed John Smith and held him down. He struggled against them. He did not understand what was happening. He thought the warriors were trying to kill him. He did not know it was a ceremony.

I watched carefully because I had a part to play in the ritual. When the biggest warrior raised his war club over John Smith's head, I threw myself over the Englishman.

"Please, Father, spare his life," I cried.

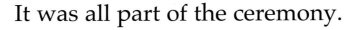

It was all part of the ceremony.

The ceremony meant Father was adopting John Smith into our tribe. "You will call me father," he told John Smith, "and I will call you son."

A few days later, John Smith returned to his own village. Father told us that John Smith had traveled so far from his village because he wanted to trade with us for food. His people came from far away, and they did not understand what food to grow to keep them fed through the winter. His people were hungry.

Father decided to send some of our people to John Smith's village with food and furs to trade. I begged him to let me go along.

"Please," I said. "I can help. John Smith trusts me."

"All right, little playful one," he said, because that is what Pocahontas means. It means little playful one.

I hugged him and ran to join the trading party. Father almost never tells me no. He has many children, but I think I am his favorite.

We took the food and furs to John Smith's village, called Jamestown. The people were glad to see us. They traded copper and tools for corn and pumpkins.

I visited Jamestown often after that. Sometimes Father sent me with messages or supplies. Sometimes I went by myself. I liked the English. I played with the boys of their village. I taught them our language, and they taught me theirs.

My favorite Englishman, though, was John Smith.

But then my people and his people stopped getting along. The Powhatans were afraid the English would try to take more land. Fighting broke out, and Father stopped sending food to Jamestown.

I could not let the English starve. I sneaked food to their village. I also told them when the Powhatans planned to attack.

One day when I went to Jamestown, John Smith was not there. His people told me he had died. It made me very sad because he was my friend.

The fighting between my people and the English grew worse. My father sent me to another Powhatan village to live. Jazapaws was the chief of that village, and he was still friendly with the English.

One day Jazapaws told me an Englishman, Captain Argall, had sailed his ship up the river. Captain Argall had invited Jazapaws to have dinner with him aboard his ship.

"He wants you to come," Jazapaws said.

That night Jazapaws took me to the ship. I looked around in wonder at its size.

"Welcome aboard the *Treasurer*," Captain Argall said.

"It was kind of you to invite me for dinner, " I said.

"You'll be staying for longer than dinner," he said.

"Are you taking me prisoner?" I asked.

"Don't think of yourself as a prisoner," said Captain Argall. "You are a guest."

"Do you keep all your guests from leaving?" I asked.

"You can leave as soon as your father returns the Englishmen he captured," the captain said. "He'll do anything to keep his favorite daughter safe. Don't worry, Pocahontas. You've been a good friend, and we'll make your stay pleasant."

Jazapaws acted surprised, but he knew exactly what was happening. Captain Argall dismissed him, and when Jazapaws reached shore, one of the captain's men handed him a kettle. Jazapaws sold me to the English for a kettle!

The *Treasurer* sailed to Jamestown. Captain Argall did his best to make me feel like a guest. I was not allowed to go back to my people, but I could move about the English settlement as I pleased.

I lived with Reverend Whitaker and his family. They gave me English clothes to wear and taught me to read and write. Mostly we read the Bible. I learned about the English religion, and in some ways, it was like mine. The English had one God. The Powhatan had many gods with one chief god. Our chief god created everything just as the English believed their God did. We believed when a person died, his soul went to a wonderful place. The English called that place heaven.

After a while, Father returned some of the prisoners, but not all. He sent word to the English to treat his daughter well, and so I stayed.

While I lived with Reverend Whitaker's family, I met John Rolfe.

John Rolfe was quiet and sincere. He spoke often of his future plans.

"I want you to be part of my future," he told me one day. "I love you, Pocahontas. I want to marry you."

When I told my father I loved John Rolfe, he agreed to the marriage. The English governor also agreed. The governor wanted peace with the Powhatan. He knew that if I married John Rolfe, my father would not attack the English.

The governor said I must be baptized a Christian before John Rolfe and I could marry. It was a big step, but I believed what Reverend Whitaker had taught me. I became a Christian and took the name Rebecca. Then I became Rebecca Rolfe.

Father did not come to the wedding. He was too proud, and it would have been too hard for him to see his daughter dressed in English clothes, saying English prayers, and accepting English ways. He sent some of my brothers, instead.

John Rolfe and I were happy together, and soon we had a son. We named him Thomas, and I loved him more than I knew was possible.

When Thomas was a year old, Captain Argall and the governor of Virginia decided to sail back to England. The governor wanted me to go, too.

John Rolfe, Thomas, and I boarded the *Treasurer* bound for England. Others of my tribe also sailed to England, including my father's advisor Tomacomo. My marriage had brought peace between the English and the Powhatan, but Father was not sure it would last. He wanted to know how many English he would face if there was ever war, so he gave Tomacomo a stick. He told Tomacomo to carve a notch in the stick for each Englishman he saw in England.

Poor Tomacomo! He frantically began notching his stick as soon as the ship landed, trying to make a mark for every person he saw. When we got to shore, Tomacomo threw the stick down in disgust. "If I mark a notch for every Englishman," he said, "there will be no stick."

Soon after we arrived, the governor said we would be presented to the court. That meant we would meet the king and queen of England! "They know you helped the Englishmen at Jamestown," John Rolfe said. "They want to meet you and the other Powhatan who sailed with us."

We dressed in our best English clothes and went to the lodge of the king and queen, which was called a palace. The palace was enormous!

The throne room, where the king and queen sat, was crowded with people. We waited until my name was called.

The king and queen asked many questions, and I told them all I could. They must have adopted me into their tribe because they took me everywhere with them. I went to plays, concerts, dinners, and balls. An artist even drew my portrait.

One day, I had a visitor. It was John Smith!

"John Smith," I exclaimed. "They told me you died!"

"I was injured and nobody expected me to survive the voyage back to England," he said, "but I'm too stubborn to die."

"Father will be glad to know," I said, and John Smith smiled at me.

I loved England, but it was hard on us. The Powhatan were not used to English diseases and damp weather. Some of my people grew sick and died. I got sick, too.

"Home," I said to John Rolfe. "I need to go home."

## – Epilogue –

Pocahontas, John Rolfe, and Thomas left for Jamestown, but before their ship sailed very far, Pocahontas became too sick to continue.
They docked in Gravesend, England, and carried Pocahontas ashore.
A doctor was called, but by then it was too late. Pocahontas died.

She never returned to her home.

# Gulliver's Travels

*Original Story by Jonathan Swift   Adapted by Lynne Suesse   Illustrated by David Wenzel*

Gulliver had recently returned from an adventure in Lilliput. In Lilliput, Gulliver was very large. The people and animals were tiny. They could fit in the palm of Gulliver's hand. When he returned home to London, people did not believe his tale.

"I can prove it," Gulliver said and showed them the tiny cows he had brought back from Lilliput.

Gulliver longed for more adventure. He wanted to go on another trip, so he joined up with the captain and crew of a ship called the *Adventure*.

During the voyage, the ship hit a mighty storm and was blown off course. When the storm passed, the captain spied land. A dozen crew members and Gulliver went to explore it. On the beach, Gulliver wandered off from the rest of the crew.

Gulliver heard shouting and turned back to see what was the matter. He could not believe what he saw. The crew members were rowing back to the ship! They were being chased by a giant!

Gulliver was afraid more giants lurked about, so he hid behind a rock. He peeked out, but he did not see the giant. He also did not see his shipmates or the ship. He knew he had been left behind.

Gulliver started to run. He ran as fast as he could until he found himself in a forest. Large, strange plants grew all around him. He thought the plants were unusual trees, but then he recognized them. The plants were huge stalks of corn!

Then Gulliver heard a rumbling sound. The ground began to shake. He saw the giant that had chased his ship! He knew he had to hide.

The giant walked toward Gulliver. His steps were long. His feet were huge. Gulliver began to feel hopeless. He would never be able to outrun the giant. The ground trembled, and Gulliver was afraid he was going to be stepped on.

The giant stopped and looked at the ground. He bent down and saw little Gulliver. He reached out, picked Gulliver up, and held him between his thumb and forefinger like Gulliver was a bug. Gulliver did not struggle. Then the giant smiled and dropped Gulliver into his shirt pocket.

The giant was a farmer, who owned the cornfield. The ride inside the farmer's pocket was stuffy, and it seemed like a long way to the farmer's house. When the giant took Gulliver out of his pocket, Gulliver took deep breaths and sneezed pocket fuzz out of his nose.

The farmer put Gulliver on the kitchen table. When the farmer's wife saw Gulliver, she screamed. The sound was so loud Gulliver had to cover his ears.

"Why did you bring a bug into my house?" asked the farmer's wife.

"He's not a bug," said the farmer.

Gulliver uncovered his ears and bowed to the farmer's wife. She stopped yelling and looked at him. She saw how polite he was and smiled.

"He's a man," said the farmer. "To think, I almost stepped on him!"

At dinner, Gulliver met the farmer's children, and they were delighted with him. Then the baby grabbed Gulliver and tried to put him in her mouth! The farmer's wife quickly rescued him.

Gulliver wiped himself dry with a napkin and sat down to eat. The farmer's wife crumbled bread and cut little pieces of meat for his meal. She served him milk in a thimble. Gulliver had trouble lifting the thimble, but he was very thirsty after all the excitement.

Of all the farmer's children, Gulliver liked the oldest daughter. She was very kind. She made him a cozy bed in a matchbox. She sewed tiny outfits for him. Gulliver liked the farmer's daughter best because she respected him as a man.

The farmer's daughter spent many hours teaching Gulliver the language of the land. It was a strange language, but Gulliver quickly learned it. He learned that the land was called Brobdingnag.

One day, the farmer took Gulliver to the marketplace to show him off. He put Gulliver on a fruit stand, and people gathered close.

"Amuse the people," the farmer said to Gulliver.

Gulliver walked around on the fruit and pretended to fight with his tiny knife. He spoke the Brobdingnag language and even sang a song. The crowd clapped.

Then the farmer took Gulliver to other cities. The daughter tried to protect Gulliver, but he still had to watch out for himself. Once, a boy shot an acorn at Gulliver's head with a slingshot. The acorn was as big as a pumpkin to Gulliver!

After a while, Gulliver got tired of performing. The wear could be seen on his little face, and the farmer's daughter worried.

Then one day, the royal court saw Gulliver perform. The queen of Brobdingnag was very fond of strange things, and she loved Gulliver.

"You must come and join my court," said the queen.

"I will if the farmer's daughter can come, too," Gulliver said.

The queen could not wait to show Gulliver to the king. "Why did you bring me a wind-up toy?" asked the king.

"He is not a toy," said the queen. "He is a man."

The king did not believe her. He called his royal scholars to inspect the little man. The scholars poked at Gulliver for a long time. Finally, they decided Gulliver really was a man.

The king told the queen she could keep Gulliver, so the queen had the royal craftsman make a box for Gulliver to live in. The box had many rooms and windows. It even had a handle for carrying.

Little things were made for Gulliver from the finest materials in the palace. He hung his clothes on pegs made from golden pins. He sat on a chair made from a velvet pin cushion. He ate from dishes that were silver buttons from the queen's favorite dress.

Gulliver liked life at the palace quite well, and he only had to perform for the queen on a few special occasions. The farmer's daughter was also treated well. She had her own special things and many servants to take care of her. She was free to roam the palace grounds, and she always took Gulliver with her.

The farmer's daughter took Gulliver out to the orchard and to the seashore for fresh air. She was very careful with him, but there were many dangers to such a tiny person. One time, a falling apple almost crushed him. Another time, the queen's dog picked him up in its mouth before the farmer's daughter could stop it.

Then one morning, the farmer's daughter was sick. She was much too ill to go outside, so Gulliver asked a servant to take him to the beach.

The servant carried Gulliver, in his box, to the seaside. Thinking Gulliver was safe, the servant left the box and took a walk along the shore. Gulliver was enjoying the view of the sea from his special house when an eagle picked up the box and flew away with it into the air!

The eagle carried the box for miles over the sea before it dropped it into the ocean. Gulliver was not sure where he was or if he would be found. Eventually, the captain of an English ship spied Gulliver's box floating in the sea. The crew had no idea what the huge box could be! They were even more amazed to find an Englishman, like themselves, inside.

Gulliver was glad to be back among people of his own size again. He told the crew all about his adventures in the place called Brobdingnag, but they did not believe his tale. To prove it, he showed them one of the queen's large, silver dress buttons.

# Swiss Family Robinson

*Original Story by Johann Wyss    Adapted by Catherine McCafferty    Illustrated by Gino d'Achille*

I feared the worst. We were far from Switzerland when a hurricane battered our ship. I stayed inside the cabin with my wife and my four young sons. Fritz was the oldest. Next oldest was Ernest, then Jack, then Franz. All of us were afraid, but my wife and I did our best to cheer our sons.

Suddenly, there was a crash. The ship struck rocks, and the shore was still far away. I heard the captain yell, "Lower the boats! Abandon ship!"

I hurried onto the deck just in time to see the last lifeboat leave without us.

"Courage!" I told my family. "We will find a way to shore."

The next morning it was calm. We built a raft from large pieces of broken wood from the ship. Carefully, each of us stepped onto it. The captain's two dogs came, too.

When we reached land, we saw no sign of the ship's captain or crew. I feared they had been lost in the storm. My family and I gave thanks for our safe return to land, although it was a very strange land. It was unlike anything we had ever seen before.

Our first task was to build a shelter. We made a tent from the sails of the ship. The boys gathered grass for our beds, and I gathered supplies that had washed ashore from the ship. Then I allowed the boys to explore the beach.

Jack did not get very far before he shouted. He danced about with something on his foot. As I got closer, I saw it was a lobster! The lobster was perfect for our dinner, and Ernest came back with oysters. Fritz even found some sea salt. My wife made a hearty soup.

We slept soundly that night because we were worn out from our day. Early the next morning, I told the family that Fritz and I would search for shipmates. The dogs came with us.

As we searched, we found some coconuts. We drank their sweet milk and ate the fruit. Later, we came upon some calabash, or gourd, trees. Still farther, we discovered sugarcane and cut some to carry back with us.

For Fritz, the best discovery of all was a little monkey. The monkey rode first on Fritz's shoulder. Then it rode on one of the dog's backs. The rest of the family was delighted with him.

Of the ship's crew, we found no one. We were truly alone and far from home. I knew we would be stranded for a very long time, perhaps forever.

The next day, my wife said, "The boys discovered some huge trees yesterday. I would like to live in one."

It was a great idea, and we began to work on a tree house right away. We built walls in the branches of a big tree. Boards from the ship became our floor. With the wood that was left, we built sturdy ladders.

At night, we slept in hammocks tied to the branches. It was very pleasant.

There were still many goods on the ship, so Fritz, Ernest, Jack and I went back to the wreck. Deep in the hold, I found the pieces of a small boat. It was better than our handmade raft, so we worked to put it together. After it was completed, we could not get it out of the ship's hold! Our axes could not break through the walls of the ship, so I sent the boys to the raft. I built a blasting charge. Then I lit a slow-burning fuse and hurried to shore with my sons.

We touched land just as we heard the explosion. Smoke burst out of the hold. As the smoke drifted away, we rowed back to the ship. To the boys' surprise, there was a hole big enough to let the new boat out.

We loaded the boat with the last of the ship's valuables.

After that, we set about making improvements to our tree house. My wife said, "I should like to be able to get home without climbing a ladder. Can you make a flight of stairs?"

It was possible if the trunk was hollow, and the boys took it upon themselves to find out. They tapped on the trunk until a swarm of bees came out. The trunk was hollow, but we could not claim it until the bees were gone.

I built a beehive out of gourds and grass. Fritz stopped up the hollow trunk so the bees could not escape. I put them to sleep by blowing pipe smoke into the trunk. When they were still, we cut a hole in the trunk and moved them to the beehive.

Then we built a magnificent winding staircase inside the hollow trunk. We even made a handrail. My wife loved it!

Then before we knew to expect it, the rainy season came. We hurried to build a shelter for the animals. We rushed to get the supplies inside.

We soon found we could not stay among the branches of the tree. We had to move inside the hollow trunk to stay dry. Many long days and nights passed. For months the skies were dark. We learned to make candles from beeswax to pass the time. We also thought of better alternatives for shelter in the next rainy season.

When the rains stopped, the boys and I went down to the shore where there were lots of large rocks. We wanted to make a rock shelter for our supplies. After many days of chipping away at a huge rock, Jack shouted, "My hammer has gone through!"

Jack had broken through to a salt cavern. We had found not only a place to keep our supplies dry but also a new home for the rainy season!

Now that we had our tree house for the summer and the salt cavern for the rainy season, we looked for a place for our growing number of animals. As we searched the island one day, Franz exclaimed, "There's snow!" I laughed and explained to my youngest son that the fluffy white stuff was not snow. It was cotton. The puffy blooms could be used for cloth, pillows, and beds.

After a while, we came to a grassy area near a brook. It was the perfect place for our animals. We built a shelter for the animals, and it was like a farm.

At that point, we had been on the island for almost a year. I had kept track in my journal. "We must celebrate the anniversary of our arrival on the island," I said.

On the day of our celebration, my wife and I were awakened by gunpowder blasts. The boys had started our celebration with a bang!

In the afternoon, we had a feast. Then I read aloud from the journal I had been keeping. We gave thanks for everything we had saved and for everything we had found. It was a good celebration.

On another day, I had an idea to build a canoe. The boys and I went looking for a very tall and very straight tree. When we found one, Fritz and I carefully removed the bark in one piece.

We shaped it into a canoe and joined the two ends with pegs. We tied ropes around it to give it a rounded shape.

When we were giving the canoe its final touches, Fritz saw something through the small telescope that we took from the ship. It made him shout. "I see a party of horsemen riding at full gallop right toward us!"

Ernest and Jack both looked through the telescope, but they could not tell what was approaching. I looked through the spyglass for a long time. What I saw made me laugh. "Those are ostriches," I told my sons. "We must try to catch one!"

The ostriches ran so quickly on their long legs that we could not keep up with them. We tried, but they were too quick. Finally Fritz managed to rope one.

"He will be the fastest runner from our stables," Jack said. "I am going to make a saddle and a bridle for him, and he will be mine to ride."

I worked with Jack to tame the ostrich. We knew the ostrich stopped moving when we covered its eyes. After some thought, I made a pair of blinkers for it. When both blinkers were open, the ostrich ran straight ahead. When they were closed, it stopped. When one or the other was closed, it turned. The idea worked very well, and soon the ostrich was tamed.

And then ten years had passed. Fritz was a man of twenty-five, and the other boys had also become fine young men.

Fritz returned from an expedition one day with startling news. His journey had taken him far. He had found an albatross with a note tied to one leg. The note read, "Save this unfortunate Englishwoman." I took the note off the bird and tied a new note to it. It read, "Do not despair. Help is near!" Then I let the albatross go.

I thought the note might be an old one, but Fritz wanted to make sure. He was off again, and we did not see him for many days.

"I found another island," he told us when he returned. "We must go there at once." We all went to the other island in the boat and followed him ashore. Fritz made his way to a leafy shelter and went inside. When he came out, he brought with him a young woman!

"Allow me to introduce Jennifer Montrose," Fritz said.

Jennifer Montrose was the daughter of a British officer. She and her father were sailing on separate ships when her ship was sunk by a storm. She had escaped on a lifeboat, but she was the only one who had survived.

Her story was similar to ours, but there was one important difference. She had made a life on her island by herself. She had no family to help her. Finally, Fritz had found her.

Jennifer joined us on our island. We traded stories of our survival, and the rainy season that year seemed to go by very quickly.

One evening, as the boys held target practice, a boom of guns answered their shots. Fritz and I set out to see who it was. We discovered a ship anchored nearby. Fritz peered through the telescope. "I see the captain, Father!" he said. "He is English. I know he is English! Just look at the flag the ship flies!"

We rowed out to meet the ship. The captain was very happy to see us. Colonel Montrose, Jennifer's father, had sent him to look for Jennifer. We welcomed him and his crew to our island and to our home.

They praised us for the fine homes we had built. Never had they expected to see trellises and balconies and stairs on a castaway house. We brought out our best dishes and served a fine meal that also impressed them.

Amid the joy and celebration, my wife and I looked at one another. Later, we talked quietly. She wanted to stay on the island. I found that I did not want to leave the home we had made either, but I knew Fritz would return to England to be with Jennifer. I wondered about my other sons.

"I would like to remain," Ernest said.

"As would I," Jack said.

When it was Franz's turn, he said, "I would like to go. It might be a good idea for one of us to go back home to Switzerland."

As the ship was to leave the next day, I gave Franz my journal. I asked him to publish it so others might learn of our story.

Through my son, the Robinson family would finally return to Switzerland.

# 20,000 Leagues Under the Sea

*Original Story by Jules Verne   Adapted by Suzanne Lieurance   Illustrated by Daniel Powers*

In 1866, Pierre Aronnax, a scientist, was amazed by a newspaper story. Seamen reported a large object at sea, which they could not identify.

"This 'enormous thing, '" Aronnax said to his trusted servant, Conseil, "is described as 'a long spindle-shaped object that often appears to light up. '"

Many more sightings of the object were reported. After reading more reports, Aronnax believed the object was something never seen before. As a scientist, Aronnax knew quite a lot about the sea. Newspaper reporters asked him for his scientific explanation of the strange sightings.

"Just because we have never seen anything like this, doesn't mean it doesn't exist," Aronnax explained. "We have not seen all the creatures that live in the depths of the sea. I'm convinced the object is a giant sea monster."

The reporters laughed at that, and the people who read the paper laughed, too. Then things got worse. The mysterious object attacked a ship. Then it attacked every ship it met. Shipping lines lost money because no one traveled by sea, and the idea of a sea monster no longer seemed laughable.

Then one day, Conseil handed Aronnax an official looking letter.

*Dear Monsieur Aronnax,*

*If you will kindly join the* Abraham Lincoln *on an expedition to find out if this mysterious object is indeed a giant sea monster, we would be most appreciative. A cabin awaits you. The ship sails tomorrow at 5:00 p.m.*

*Very cordially yours,*
*J.B. Hobson,*
*Secretary of Marine*

The next day, Aronnax and Conseil boarded the *Abraham Lincoln,* where they met the ship's captain, Commander Farragut.

"I've sworn to rid the seas of this wicked creature," said Commander Farragut.

Aronnax pointed to the harpoons on deck and said, "I hear Ned Land is aboard. They call him the prince of harpooners. He'll take care of the monster."

"I certainly will," said a man behind them. He extended his hand and introduced himself as Ned Land.

"Any creature able to withstand the pressure far below the sea would have to be quite strong," Aronnax said to Land.

"It would have to be made of iron plates, like an armored ship," Land said.

The *Abraham Lincoln* sailed and spent several quiet months at sea. There were no signs of any monster. After a while, the crew grew restless.

"If the monster does not appear in three days," Commander Farragut said, "we'll head for home."

The crew of the *Abraham Lincoln* scoured the seas for three more days. It found nothing until the evening of the third day.

"On the port quarter!" shouted Ned Land. "That's it!"

A blackish body emerged above the waves. The *Abraham Lincoln* charged after the creature. Everyone cheered. Ned Land stood on deck, holding his harpoon, but the ship could not move fast enough to keep up with the creature.

The cannon was loaded, and a shot was fired. It fell several feet from the creature. Another shot was fired and it hit the beast, but the creature did not seem to feel it. Then the thing disappeared under the waves.

Late that night, a huge light appeared about three miles from the *Abraham Lincoln*. The *Abraham Lincoln* moved toward the light. Ned Land held his harpoon. His arm straightened, and the harpoon flew. It made a clinking sound as it hit the creature, like metal hitting metal. The light went out and the creature charged at the ship. When the *Abraham Lincoln* was struck, Aronnax was thrown overboard.

Arronax began to sink, but something grabbed him and pulled him to the surface.

"Hold on, sir," said Conseil.

Aronnax coughed and held on to Conseil.

"Help! Help!" Land called from a distance.

Conseil and Aronnax swam toward him. Aronnax tired quickly. He fainted, and his body landed on something solid. When he came to, Conseil and Ned Land were beside him.

"We're on the top of some sort of boat," said Land.

The object made a loud grinding noise, and an iron plate moved. A man appeared but quickly disappeared. Then more men, with masked faces, appeared. They dragged Aronnax, Conseil, and Land into the strange boat and threw them into a dark prison.

Later, light came into the prison, and a man came in.

"You are aboard the *Nautilus*. I am the commander, Captain Nemo," said the man.

"We were aboard the *Abraham Lincoln*," said Aronnax. "We thought this vessel was a huge sea monster. We meant you no harm."

"That doesn't matter," said Nemo. "Since you now know about the *Nautilus*, you are my prisoners, and you will always remain my prisoners."

"You mean we will never see our families, friends, or our countries again?" asked Aronnax.

"Never," said Nemo. "But you are free to move around the *Nautilus* as you like. If you try to escape, I will kill you. No one must know about me. It isn't you that I guard. I guard myself."

Nemo turned and left, but later that night, the prisoners ate dinner with him.

"This food is delicious, Captain," said Aronnax, "but I'm not familiar with it."

"I have given up the food of the land," said Nemo.

"You mean all these foods come from the sea?" asked Aronnax.

"Yes," said Nemo. "The sea supplies me with everything."

After dinner, Nemo showed the prisoners around the *Nautilus*. The men followed him toward a library. There were wide shelves full of bound books, and electric light flooded the passageway.

"Read anything you like," said Nemo as he left them.

"I never imagined electric lighting like this," said Land. "And to think! It's all aboard a ship that can travel to the bottom of the sea."

"But why would Nemo decide to live like this and give up everything on land?" asked Conseil.

"This ship is equipped with everything one could ever need," said Aronnax. "It's as if Nemo is on some sort of mission to live this way."

The *Nautilus* traveled to places Aronnax had only read about. The men were very surprised that Nemo allowed them to explore the remote islands by themselves.

Conseil, Land, and Aronnax used a small rowboat to make their way to one of the islands. The men found breadfruit, mangoes, and pineapples. They even trapped some wood pigeons to roast. By afternoon, they had a feast.

Just as they were finishing their meal, they heard noises. Twenty natives, armed with bows, came out of the trees. The men jumped in the rowboat and rowed back to the *Nautilus*. The natives followed in canoes.

"Captain!" Aronnax yelled when they reached the *Nautilus*. "Some natives spotted us on the island. They are quickly approaching!"

"Those savages can't possibly harm us," said Nemo, "and the *Nautilus* is indestructible."

"They're going to come aboard, sir!" Conseil said.

"Let them try," said Nemo.

One of the port lids opened, and the faces of a few of the natives appeared. When the first put his hand on the ladder, he was struck by an invisible force. He screamed and let go. The same thing happened to every native who tried to enter the *Nautilus*. The ladder was charged by an electric cable. The natives received a surprising shock!

After the natives finally left, the *Nautilus* approached some underwater caves. Aronnax worried that the vessel might not really be indestructible. He had heard stories about giant squids.

"Are the stories about giant squids true?" asked Conseil.

"Such creatures do exist," said Aronnax. "One was seen here a few years ago."

"Did it have eight long tentacles?" asked Conseil.

"Yes," Aronnax said.

Conseil shuddered and pointed toward a porthole. Aronnax looked and saw such a giant squid swimming toward them. It wrapped itself around the *Nautilus*.

"Its tentacles are wrapped around the blades of the vessel," Captain Nemo said. "We can't go anywhere, except to the surface, until we get them off."

When the *Nautilus* reached the surface, Captain Nemo and Land went out on deck. They had axes and harpoons to attack the monster, but the giant squid attacked them, instead. It trapped Nemo with one of its giant tentacles. Land harpooned it until it let Nemo go. Then the squid's huge beak opened over Land's head. Nemo shoved his axe into the monster's mouth. Land moved and grabbed another harpoon. He stabbed it into the monster's eye. Finally, the squid died.

The men had been Nemo's prisoners for over seven months when the *Nautilus* neared the United States. As they approached the coast of New York, another vessel came into view. It was a warship.

"Prepare to sink it," Nemo called down from the deck. "War destroys lives, so war must be destroyed!"

"That explains the Captain's mission," said Aronnax. "It seems he's at war against anything related to war. It's vengeance."

"When the *Abraham Lincoln* made it back to port, word must have spread that the giant sea monster is actually a submarine vessel," said Land.

The men heard an explosion and rushed on deck. The warship was sinking.

The *Nautilus* escaped to the dangerous coast of Norway. There, waters rushed with such speed that ships and even whales had been destroyed.

"We need to escape before Nemo gets us killed," said Land.

When the vessel surfaced, Aronnax, Conseil, and Ned Land had a plan. They boarded the rowboat and set off. No one prevented them because no one would have expected them to go into such rough water in a rowboat. Surprisingly, they made it to shore with the help of a coastal fisherman.

The three men never learned what happened to the *Nautilus*.

Captain Nemo was never seen or heard from again.

# The Three Muskateers

*Original Story by Alexandre Dumas    Adapted by Suzanne Lieurance    Illustrated by John Lund*

D'artagnan was eighteen, and it was time for him to make his way in the world. "I have little to give you, " said d'Artagnan's father, "except fifty gold coins, this letter to Captain Treville, and my prized horse."

D'Artagnan accepted the coins and the letter, but he was going to look silly riding the old nag even though it had been his father's most valued steed.

"Treville is captain of the musketeers," continued his father. "Go to him with the letter. Become a musketeer."

D'Artagnan's greatest wish was to join the musketeers, the soldiers who guarded the king of France, so he mounted the old horse and started for Paris. When he stopped at an inn, a man with a scar laughed at his horse.

"No one laughs at my horse, sir," d'Artagnan said.

The man with the scar laughed harder, so d'Artagnan lunged at him. The man with the scar hit d'Artagnan on the head, and d'Artagnan fell to the ground.

The man with the scar found d'Artagnan's letter addressed to Captain Treville. "He is trying to ruin my plan!" he said to himself as he put the letter in his pocket.

When d'Artagnan came to, the man with the scar was talking with a woman. He called her Milady de Winter. She called him Count Rochefort. "I'm leaving for Paris," said the count. "The cardinal wants you to go back to England where you can spy on the duke of Buckingham."

D'Artagnan arrived in Paris and went to Captain Treville's office. Treville was speaking with two men. Their names were Porthos and Aramis. "The cardinal told me that three of my men started a riot yesterday," said Treville.

"Sir, I can explain," said Porthos. "The cardinal's guards attacked us. Athos was wounded. We fought well and escaped."

Just then, Athos came into the office. He had a bandaged arm. "You sent for me, sir?" he asked.

"Yes, Athos," Treville said. "I was saying that musketeers should not risk their lives needlessly." Athos nodded. Then the three musketeers left.

Treville asked d'Artagnan why he had come. "I want to be a musketeer," said d'Artagnan. "I had a letter from my father, but a coward with a scar attacked me and took it." Treville shook his head and told d'Artagnan that he must train as a regular soldier before he would be ready to guard the king.

Through the window, d'Artagnan saw Count Rochefort. D'Artagnan ran from the office to catch the count, but on the stairs, he bumped into Athos and his injured arm. "The convent at noon!" said Athos angrily, challenging d'Artagnan to a duel.

D'Artagnan raced on and came upon Porthos. He tried to get by Porthos, but he got tangled up in Porthos's cloak. "The convent at noon!" said Porthos angrily.

D'Artagnan hurried on and ran past Aramis. He accidentally stepped on Aramis's foot. "The convent at noon!" said Aramis angrily.

D'Artagnan did not find the count, so he went to the convent at noon. Athos, Porthos, and Aramis were already there. D'Artagnan knew musketeers were highly trained. He would lose a duel with any one of them, but he drew his sword anyway.

"Put your sword away," whispered Porthos.

It was too late. Four of the cardinal's guards appeared. "You are all under arrest for breaking the cardinal's rule against dueling!" one of the guards shouted.

"There are four of them and only three of us," said Athos.

"There are four of us, not three," d'Artagnan said. Then the four lunged at the guards. When the guards were defeated, Athos, Porthos, Aramis, and d'Artagnan went away arm in arm. D'Artagnan felt like his greatest wish was coming true!

Captain Treville heard about the musketeers' battle. He scolded them, but he also said, "I know the cardinal's guards picked the quarrel with you."

The king was pleased with them, too. The cardinal was the king's advisor, but the king did not like the cardinal. He enjoyed it when the cardinal was defeated. He summoned Athos, Porthos, Aramis, and d'Artagnan to the palace.

"You are the young man who fought so well with my musketeers," said the king to d'Artagnan. "Here are one hundred gold pieces as a reward."

"Thank you, Sire," d'Artagnan said and bowed to the king.

D'Artagnan felt rich! First he bought a fine meal for his friends. Next he hired a servant to work for him. Then he rented an apartment. But quickly, all the gold was spent.

D'Artagnan's landlord, Beaufort, paid him a visit. He asked d'Artagnan for his help. Beaufort's wife, Constance, had been kidnapped.

"My wife works for the queen," said Beaufort. "The duke of Buckingham is in love with the queen. The cardinal knows this, so he spies on them. The queen is loyal to the king and feels only friendship for the duke, but the cardinal does not believe it. The cardinal is out to ruin the queen. Because the queen trusts my wife, the cardinal thinks my wife knows the queen's secrets. I think a man with a scar kidnapped her."

"Count Rochefort!" d'Artagnan said.

"Rescue my wife," said Beaufort. "In return, I won't ask for rent, and I can pay fifty gold pieces."

D'Artagnan agreed to help, and Beaufort left. But outside, four of the cardinal's guards arrested Beaufort. D'Artagnan could not help Beaufort because the guards would have arrested him, too. He could not rescue Constance if he was in prison.

Later, d'Artagnan heard voices. Beaufort's apartment was just below his apartment, and he heard Beaufort's wife, Constance, pleading with the cardinal's guards.

D'Artagnan reached for his sword, rushed down to the apartment, and knocked on the door. When it opened, he rushed inside. He fought very bravely, and the cardinal's guards fled in all directions.

"I must get back to the palace," said Constance. "The queen needs me."

Eventually, the cardinal set Beaufort free. Beaufort went happily home.

Then the cardinal called for Count Rochefort. Rochefort told him the queen and the duke had been seen together in London. The queen had even given the duke the sash with the twelve diamonds on it that the king had given to her as a gift.

"I shall write to Milady de Winter in London," said the cardinal, "and tell her to steal two of the diamonds and bring them to me. The queen will be disgraced!"

Later, the cardinal went to the king. He suggested the king give a royal ball so the queen could wear her new diamond sash. The king thought it was a fine idea.

"I gave the diamond sash to the duke as a gift," the queen said to Constance when she heard about the ball. "The cardinal knows and plans to disgrace me."

"Write a letter to the duke and explain about the diamond sash," said Constance. "My husband will deliver the letter and bring the sash back."

The queen gave Constance the letter. Then she pulled a ring from her finger. "It is worth a thousand gold coins," said the queen. "Give it to your husband to pay for his trip."

Constance rushed home. "Help me," she said to her husband. "Take this letter to the duke, and you will earn a thousand gold coins."

"That would make the cardinal angry," Beaufort said.

"Never mind," Constance said. She knew she could no longer trust her husband.

Beaufort stormed out. Then d'Artagnan arrived. "I heard everything!" he said. "Athos, Porthos, Aramis, and I will deliver the letter to the duke."

D'Artagnan went to Captain Treville and asked that Athos, Porthos, and Aramis be allowed to join him on a mission to save the queen's honor.

"Of course," said Treville. "I will give each of them leave to join you."

D'Artagnan collected his three friends, and they rode to Calais. They stopped at an inn to eat. A man at the next table raised his glass and toasted the cardinal.

"And a toast to the king," said Porthos.

The man refused to drink to the king, and that made Porthos angry. He argued with the man, but there was no time for a fight. D'Artagnan, Athos, and Aramis had to leave Porthos to duel with the man by himself. Later, they passed some men on the road, and the men began firing at them. Aramis was injured, and they had to stop at another inn because he could not continue the journey. Athos quarreled so long with the innkeeper over money, d'Artagnan had to leave without him, too.

D'Artagnan arrived in Calais alone. He went straight to the ship bound for England. There he saw the ship's captain talking to Count Rochefort!

D'Artagnan followed the count. Then he charged the count and tackled him. They wrestled, and the count was knocked down. D'Artagnan ran and boarded the ship just as it set sail.

When the ship arrived in England, d'Artagnan went to the duke of Buckingham and gave him the queen's letter.

The duke read the letter. Then he got the queen's diamond sash and examined it.

"Two of the diamonds are gone!" he said. "I only wore the sash once, and Milady de Winter was with me! She must have stolen the diamonds for the cardinal!"

71

The duke sent for his jeweler. The duke explained that he needed two identical diamonds by the next morning. The jeweler nodded and went quickly away.

The next morning, d'Artagnan traveled back to France with the sash and new diamonds. He arrived just as the ball was beginning. When the king and queen entered the room, the cardinal handed a box to the king. Inside were two diamonds.

"The queen is missing two diamonds from her sash, Sire," said the cardinal.

The king counted the diamonds on the queen's sash. "All twelve diamonds are here," the king said to the cardinal. "What does this mean?"

The cardinal saw d'Artagnan and realized he had been outsmarted. "It means I wish to present these diamonds to the queen," lied the cardinal.

"It was d'Artagnan who ruined your plan," Milady whispered to the cardinal. "But look at d'Artagnan and Constance. He likes her. We can use her against him."

"How?" asked the cardinal. "My spies tell me the queen is sending Constance away."

"I will take care of her," said Milady. "Just give me permission to do anything for the good of France."

The cardinal wrote Milady a letter.

Later, Milady met Count Rochefort on the street. Neither of them saw d'Artagnan's servant. The servant heard the count say Constance was safe at the convent. He heard Milady say she would go there. The servant rushed to tell d'Artagnan.

D'Artagnan found Athos, Porthos, and Aramis. They had to get to the convent before Milady de Winter!

Milady de Winter went to the convent and asked for Constance Beaufort. To put Constance at ease, she made up a lie. She told Constance that d'Artagnan was coming to keep her company.

"I'm so excited to see d'Artagnan!" Constance said.

"Have a glass of wine to calm yourself," said Milady.

Milady turned away to pour the wine and quickly dropped some poison into Constance's glass. Constance raised the glass to drink, and d'Artagnan burst into the room. "It's poison!" d'Artagnan yelled. "Don't drink it!"

Constance dropped the glass to the floor. D'Artagnan went to Milady and tore the cardinal's letter from her pocket. He smiled when he read it.

Then d'Artagnan and the three musketeers took Milady to the cardinal.

"I have your permission to punish Milady for her crimes," d'Artagnan said.

"My permission?" the cardinal asked. "How can that be?"

D'Artagnan read from the letter he had taken from Milady. "'The bearer of this letter acts under my orders for the good of France.' It was signed by you, Cardinal."

The cardinal took his pen and wrote something on another sheet of paper. Then he handed it to d'Artagnan.

D'Artagnan turned to Athos, Porthos, and Aramis.

"I'm a musketeer!" he said. "My greatest wish has come true!"

# Anne of Green Gables

*Original Story by L. M. Montgomery    Adapted by Rebecca Grazulis    Illustrated by Kathy Mitchell*

Has the five-thirty train come?" Matthew asked the station master. "Come and gone, sir," replied the station master, "but there was a passenger dropped off for you. A little girl. She's outside."

"But I'm expecting a boy," said Matthew nervously.

"You'd better explain things to her," the station master said.

Matthew sighed and walked down the platform. He was a shy man, and talking to people was not easy for him.

The girl was eleven years old and had red hair. She wore an old dress and a faded brown sailor hat, but her eyes were bright.

"Are you Mr. Matthew Cuthbert of Green Gables?" she asked. "I was afraid you weren't coming. I was about to climb into that cherry tree all white with bloom."

Matthew could not tell this girl with the glowing eyes that there had been a mistake.

"I'm sorry I'm late," said Matthew softly.

"That's okay," said the girl. "I'm very glad you've come. It's wonderful I'm going to live with you. I've never belonged to anybody before."

As Matthew began the drive to Green Gables, the girl broke off a branch of cherry blossoms when it brushed against the side of the buggy.

"This is the bloomiest place!" she said.

Matthew was quiet, but the girl continued to chatter.

"Am I talking too much?" she asked. "I can stop, but it's hard."

"You can talk as much as you like," Matthew said. "I really don't mind."

"Is there a brook anywhere near Green Gables?" asked the girl.

"Well, yes," said Matthew, "there's one right below the house."

"I've always wanted to live near a brook," she said. "It would make me happy, but I can't be exactly perfectly happy because… well, what color is this?"

The girl held up one of her braids to show Matthew.

"It's red, right?" he said.

"Yes, red," she said. "Now you see why I can never be exactly perfectly happy. Red hair will be my lifelong sorrow."

Soon Matthew was rounding the curve that led to Green Gables.

"That's Green Gables, isn't it?" she asked, pointing.

"You've guessed it," said Matthew.

"As soon as I saw it, I knew it was home!" she said.

Matthew stirred uneasily in his seat. He knew what was coming. He could see Marilla, his sister, standing on the porch. She was staring hard at him.

"Matthew Cuthbert, who's that?" Marilla asked. "Where is the boy?"

"There wasn't any boy," said Matthew. "There was only her."

"This is a pretty piece of business!" Marilla said and went into the house.

The girl followed Marilla into the kitchen. Then she burst into tears.

"You don't want me!" she cried. "You don't want me because I'm not a boy!"

She sat at the table, buried her face in her hands, and cried. Marilla and Matthew looked at each other. Neither knew what to do.

"There's no need to cry," said Marilla.

"There is!" The girl said. "You would cry, too, if you were an orphan and came to a place you thought was going to be home and found out they didn't want you!"

"Well, don't cry," said Marilla. "You'll stay here tonight. What is your name?"

"Anne," said the girl, "but Anne is such an unromantic name."

"Fiddlesticks!" said Marilla. "Anne is a very sensible name."

"Well, then," said the girl, "please call me Anne spelled with an e. If you'll call me Anne spelled with an e, I shall try to live with it."

"Very well, Anne with an e," said Marilla.

Soon Matthew and Marilla sat down to supper with their guest, but Anne only nibbled some bread.

"You're not eating anything," said Marilla.

"Can *you* eat when you're in the depths of despair?" Anne asked.

"I've never been in the depths of despair," said Marilla.

"Please don't be mad because I can't eat," said Anne.

"I guess she's tired," said Matthew. "Best put her to bed."

Marilla lit a candle and led Anne upstairs to the east gable bedroom.

"Undress and get into bed," said Marilla. "I'll be back shortly for the candle."

Anne did as she was told. With a sob, she got into bed. Marilla soon came back. She picked up the candle and stood at the doorway.

"Good night," she said.

"How can you say good night when it is the very worst night I've ever had in my whole life?" she asked.

Marilla did not know what to say, so she closed the door and went downstairs.

"Fine kettle of fish," she said.

"I suppose so," said Matthew sadly.

"You suppose so?" asked Marilla.

"Well, she's a nice little thing," said Matthew. "It's a pity to send her back."

"You want to keep her!" exclaimed Marilla. "What good would she be to us?"

"Marilla," Matthew said. "We might be some good to her."

Anne cried herself to sleep that night, but when she woke the next morning and saw the blossoms of the cherry tree outside her window, she smiled. She did not notice when Marilla entered the room.

"It's time you were dressed," Marilla said.

"Oh, isn't it wonderful?" Anne asked.

"It's a big tree," said Marilla, "but the fruit doesn't amount to much."

"Not just the tree," said Anne. "I mean the whole world. I can never be in the depths of despair in the morning. Isn't it splendid that there are mornings?"

"Get dressed and never mind," said Marilla.

"The world is not as bad as it was last night," Anne said at the breakfast table. "I'm glad it's a sunshiny morning, but I like rainy mornings, too. All mornings are interesting, don't you think?"

"You talk too much for a little girl," said Marilla. "Why don't you go outside until lunchtime?"

Anne ran to the door but stopped short.

"What's the matter now?" asked Marilla.

"There is no use loving Green Gables," said Anne. "If I go out and meet it, I won't be able to help loving it. What is the name of the geranium on the windowsill?"

"That's the apple-scented geranium," said Marilla.

"Not that kind of name," Anne said.

"I mean a name you gave it yourself. Maybe it hurts a geranium's feelings just to be called a geranium," said Anne.

Later that day, Marilla and Anne set out for the orphanage. Anne was quiet, which was unusual.

"Tell me what you know about yourself," said Marilla. "How old are you?"

"I was eleven last March," said Anne. "My father's name was Walter. My mother's name was Bertha. Aren't Walter and Bertha lovely names?"

"It doesn't matter what a person's name is as long as he behaves," said Marilla.

"I read once that a rose by any other name would smell as sweet, but I don't know," Anne said. "How could a rose be as nice if it was called skunk cabbage?"

Marilla tried not to laugh.

"Anyway," said Anne, "my parents died when I was three months old."

"Where did you go?" Marilla asked sadly.

"Mrs. Thomas took me in," said Anne. "When she died, I lived with Mrs. Hammond. When Mrs. Hammond died, I went to the orphanage."

Marilla did not ask any more questions. It no longer mattered if the orphanage made a mistake. Marilla would take Anne home for a while.

Marilla took Anne up to bed that night.

"Last night, you didn't say your prayers," said Marilla.

"I never say prayers," said Anne.

"Don't you know you should say your prayers?" asked Marilla.

"Mrs. Thomas told me God made my hair red, and I've never cared for Him since," said Anne. "I'll say my prayers if it pleases you, but you'll have to tell me what to say."

"Kneel down by the bed," said Marilla.

"Why do people kneel to pray?" asked Anne. "If I really wanted to pray I'd go out to a big field and look up into the sky. What next?"

"Just thank God for your blessings and ask Him humbly for the things you want," said Marilla.

"Heavenly Father," began Anne, "I thank thee for Green Gables. That's all the blessings I can think of just now. I want a lot of things, but I'll only say the most important one. Please let me stay at Green Gables. Yours respectfully, Anne."

Anne paused and then looked at Marilla.

"Did I do it right?" she asked.

Marilla did not know what to say, so she just tucked Anne into bed.

"Oh, I should have said 'Amen' like they do in church," said Anne. "Do you think it will make any difference?"

"I don't suppose it will," said Marilla. "Now, good night."

Before Anne came downstairs the next morning, Marilla talked to Matthew.

"Anne may stay, Matthew," said Marilla. "I'll do my best to bring her up."

"I knew you'd see it like that," Matthew said. "She is an interesting little thing."

"It'd be better if she was a useful little thing," said Marilla.

When Anne came into the room, she was shaking from head to foot.

"Are you going to send me away, then?" asked Anne.

"Matthew and I have decided to keep you," said Marilla.

"I'm crying," said Anne. "I can't think why. I'm glad, but glad doesn't seem the right word. It's something more than glad. Why am I crying?"

"You're all worked up," said Marilla. "Sit down and calm yourself."

"What am I to call you?" asked Anne. "Can I call you Aunt Marilla?"

"You'll call me just plain Marilla," said Marilla.

"I'd love to call you Aunt Marilla," said Anne. "It would make me feel as if I really belonged to you."

"I'm not your aunt, so it wouldn't be fair," Marilla said. "We will be friends."

Anne smiled. Then she looked up at Matthew and Marilla.

"Oh, I'm so happy to be Anne of Green Gables!" she said.

# The Jungle Book

*Original Story by Rudyard Kipling    Adapted by Lora Kalkman    Illustrated by Sarah Dillard*

It was a warm evening in the jungle. The Wolf family heard a purring sound nearby. It was the tiger, Shere Kahn, and he was hunting. The wolf family waited quietly. Then the tiger growled, and the wolves knew he had pounced. The growl was followed by a loud yelp of pain.

"That foolish tiger missed his target," Father Wolf said.

Then the wolves heard a rustle of leaves. An intruder was headed for their den. Father Wolf crouched down, ready to pounce. Then the intruder emerged from the bushes. Father Wolf was surprised to see that it was a baby boy!

"It is a man cub," Father Wolf said. "He's just a little fellow."

The child had soft brown skin and big brown eyes. He was not wearing a stitch of clothing, and he looked like he had just learned to walk.

"He's lost," Mother Wolf said. "It is a wonder that Shere Kahn did not kill him."

The baby boy smiled and laughed at the two wolves.

"Every baby needs a mother," Mother Wolf said. "I will take care of him. We will call him Mowgli."

"Very well," Father Wolf said. "I'll announce it at our next pack meeting."

When the wolves and all the other animals had gathered at Council Rock, Father Wolf told them about Mowgli.

"Turn the man cub over to me," Shere Kahn said angrily. "He is my prey."

"We need two votes to allow Mowgli to live with the pack," said Akela, the wolf leader, ignoring Shere Kahn.

"I vote yes," said Baloo, the brown bear.

"I also vote yes," said Bagheera, the black panther.

"It is settled, then," said Akela. "The man cub stays."

So it was that Mowgli grew up in the jungle. He played with his wolf brothers. He learned many things from his friends, Baloo and Bagheera. The jungle was his home.

Then when Mowgli was eleven years old, Bagheera came to warn him of danger.

"Mowgli," said the panther, "Shere Kahn is still out to get you. He has convinced many wolves that you should not live in the jungle. The wolves are afraid you will hurt them one day."

"I would never hurt anyone," said Mowgli.

"I know that," said Bagheera, "but you must do as I say. Go to the man village and fetch a pot with fire inside. Shere Kahn and his friends are afraid of fire. Keep it burning with sticks. Then bring it to Council Rock tonight when the pack meets."

Mowgli did as he was told and went to the nearby man village. He saw animals grazing and children playing. He also saw men and women using fire.

Mowgli hid behind some bushes and waited until no one was looking. Then he grabbed a black pot with red fire inside and ran back to the jungle. He kept the fire going by adding new sticks to it, until Bagheera came to get him.

"Akela is getting old," said Bagheera. "Many wolves want Shere Kahn to lead the pack. They will make him the leader tonight. Then Shere Kahn will surely kill you. Use the fire to save yourself. Then head for the man village. You must live there until it is safe."

Mowgli did not want to leave the jungle, but when they arrived at Council Rock, Mowgli saw that Bagheera was right.

"Let me have the man cub," roared Shere Kahn. "No man belongs here."

The wolves surrounded Mowgli. Shere Kahn licked his lips.

Mowgli grabbed a branch and dipped it into the red fire. The branch caught fire, and Mowgli waved the flaming stick at his enemies.

"Back!" he yelled. "Stay back, or I will burn you!"

The animals were terrified and backed away.

"Hear this," Mowgli said. "I will leave the jungle for now, but one day I will return. I will come back with Shere Kahn's hide, Akela will be restored as the rightful leader of the pack, and we will have peace in the jungle again."

Mowgli set out for the man village. When he got there, the village people stared at him.

One kind woman took Mowgli to her hut. She understood that he was not like other boys his age. From her, Mowgli learned the ways of the man village.

"Mowgli, other boys your age have tasks," his new mother said. "Your task will be to herd the cattle in the fields. Each day, you must lead all of the cattle to the pasture to graze. When the sun sets at night, you must lead all of the animals back to the village."

Mowgli was glad to have the chance to go to the fields. The fields were next to the jungle, and he missed the jungle.

One day, after Mowgli had led the animals to the field, he sat under a tree to rest. Gazing toward the jungle, he saw Grey Wolf Brother. He was sitting on a rock. Mowgli ran to his brother.

"I have important news for you," Grey Wolf Brother said. "Shere Kahn is the leader of the pack now. He has vowed to kill you. Look for me on this rock each day. If you do not see me, it means Shere Kahn plans to attack."

"If I do not see you here on this rock," Mowgli said, "I will meet you at the edge of the ravine."

Every morning, Mowgli spotted Grey Wolf Brother lying on the rock. Then one morning, the rock was bare. Mowgli raced to the edge of the ravine.

The ravine was a giant hole in the jungle, with steep walls. The walls were very difficult to climb. Mowgli found Grey Wolf Brother waiting for him.

"Shere Kahn plans to kill you tonight," Grey Wolf Brother said.  "We must move swiftly. He has just eaten, and he is sleeping at the bottom of the ravine."

"I have an idea," Mowgli said. "We can scare the cattle. They will stampede and run into the ravine. Shere Kahn will be trapped. He will be trampled."

Grey Wolf Brother thought it was a good plan, but he did not think the cattle would be afraid of Mowgli. He wondered how he would manage alone.

"I can help scare the cattle," a voice said.

It was Akela! He had come to help.

The wolves began to howl to scare the cattle. The cattle began to run, causing a stampede. Grey Wolf Brother and Akela chased the cattle into the ravine.

Shere Kahn was awakened by the thundering noise. He opened his eyes just in time to see the cattle racing toward him.

Just as Mowgli had planned, the cattle trampled Shere Kahn.

Mowgli skinned the tiger and draped the striped hide over his shoulders.

He went back to the village. The villagers feared the ferocious tiger, so Mowgli thought they would be pleased. But the villagers were afraid. They did not understand how such a young boy could slay such a large tiger. They threw rocks at him and ordered him to leave the village. Sadly, he left the man village.

Mowgli headed back to the jungle with Shere Kahn's skin on his back. He stopped at his family's den. Father Wolf, Mother Wolf, and his brothers were happy to see him. Baloo and Bagheera were glad to see him, too.

"It is time for me to return to Council Rock," Mowgli said. "I will take Shere Kahn's hide, as I promised, and lay it upon the rock for all to see."

Mowgli's brothers ran ahead to summon all the jungle animals to Council Rock. When Mowgli arrived with Baloo and Bagheera, everyone was there. Triumphantly, Mowgli climbed Council Rock and spread out Shere Kahn's skin.

"Because I have slain Shere Kahn, the tiger, I can choose the next leader," said Mowgli. "Akela will be restored as the rightful leader of the pack."

Akela smiled. All of the animals cheered. Thanks to Mowgli, there was peace in the jungle again.

# Paul Revere's Ride

*Written by Henry Wadsworth Longfellow    Illustrated by Jon Goodell*

Listen, my children, and you shall hear
Of the midnight ride of Paul Revere,
On the eighteenth of April, in Seventy-five;
Hardly a man is now alive
Who remembers that famous day and year.

He said to his friend, "If the British march
By land or sea from the town tonight,
Hang a lantern aloft in the belfry arch
Of the North Church tower as a signal light —
One, if by land, or two, if by sea;
And I on the opposite shore will be,
Ready to ride and spread the alarm
Through every Middlesex village and farm,
For the country folk to be up and to arm."

Then he said, "Good night!" and with muffled oar
Silently rowed to the Charlestown shore,
Just as the moon rose over the bay,
Where swinging wide at her moorings lay
The *Somerset*, British man-of-war;
A phantom ship, with each mast and spar
Across the moon like a prison bar,
And a huge black hulk, that was magnified
By its own reflection in the tide.

Meanwhile, his friend, through alley and street,
Wanders and watches with eager ears,
Till in silence around him he hears
The muster of men at the barrack door,
The sound of arms, and the tramp of feet,
And the measured tread of the grenadiers,
Marching down to their boats on the shore.

Then he climbed to the tower of the Old North Church,
By the wooden stairs, with stealthy tread,
To the belfry-chamber overhead,
And startled the pigeons from their perch
On the sombre rafters, that round him made
Masses and moving shapes of shade,
Up the trembling ladder, steep and tall,
To the highest window in the wall,
Where he paused to listen and look down
A moment on the roofs of the town,
And the moonlight flowing over all.

Beneath, in the churchyard, lay the dead,
In their night-encampment on the hill,
Wrapped in silence so deep and still
That he could hear, like a sentinel's tread,
The watchful night-wind, as it went
Creeping along from tent to tent,
And seeming to whisper, "All is well!"
A moment only he feels the spell
Of the place and the hour, and the secret dread
Of the lonely belfry and the dead;
For suddenly all his thoughts are bent
On a shadowy something far away,
Where the river widens to meet the bay,
A line of black that bends and floats
On the rising tide, like a bridge of boats.

Meanwhile, impatient to mount and ride,
Booted and spurred, with a heavy stride
On the opposite shore walked Paul Revere.
Now he patted his horse's side,
Now gazed at the landscape far and near,
Then, impetuous, stamped the earth,
And turned and tightened his saddle girth;
But mostly he watched with eager search
The belfry-tower of the Old North Church,
As it rose above the graves on the hill,
Lonely and spectral and sombre and still.
And lo! as he looks, on the belfry's height
A glimmer, and then a gleam of light!
He springs to the saddle, the bridle he turns,
But lingers and gazes, till full on his sight
A second lamp in the belfry burns!

A hurry of hoofs in a village street,
A shape in the moonlight, a bulk in the dark,
And beneath, from the pebbles, in passing, a spark
Struck out by a steed flying fearless and fleet;
That was all! And yet, through the gloom and the light,
The fate of a nation was riding that night;
And the spark struck out by that steed, in his flight,
Kindled the land into flame with its heat.

It was twelve by the village clock,
When he crossed the bridge into Medford town.
He heard the crowing of the cock,
And the barking of the farmer's dog,
And felt the damp of the river fog,
That rises after the sun goes down.

It was one by the village clock,
When he galloped into Lexington.
He saw the gilded weathercock
Swim in the moonlight as he passed,
And the meetinghouse windows, blank and bare,
Gaze at him with a spectral glare,
As if they already stood aghast
At the bloody work they would look upon.

It was two by the village clock,
When he came to the bridge in Concord town.
He heard the bleating of the flock,
And the twitter of the birds among the trees,
And felt the breath of the morning breeze
Blowing over the meadows brown.
And one was safe and asleep in his bed
Who at the bridge would be first to fall,
Who that day would be lying dead,
Pierced by a British musket ball.

You know the rest. In the books you have read,
How the British Regulars fired and fled,
How the farmers gave them ball for ball,
From behind each fence and farmyard wall,
Chasing the redcoats down the lane,
Then crossing the fields to emerge again
Under the trees at the turn of the road,
And only pausing to fire and load.

So through the night rode Paul Revere;
And so through the night went his cry of alarm
To every Middlesex village and farm —
A cry of defiance and not of fear,
A voice in the darkness, a knock at the door,
And a word that shall echo forevermore!
For, borne on the night-wind of the Past,
Through all our history, to the last,
In the hour of darkness and peril and need,
The people will waken and listen to hear
The hurrying hoofbeats of that steed,
And the midnight message of Paul Revere.